# The Snorgh and the Sailor

ALISON GREEN BOOKS

By Will Buckingham

Illustrated by Thomas Docherty

The Snorgh lived alone, in an ugly little house on the marsh. Every day he snuffled along the shoreline, picking samphire to make soup. His webbed feet sank into the mud and the wind made lonely sounds as it came from the sea.

Every evening the Snorgh huddled
in his chair by the fire.

"How lucky I am," he muttered, "to have nobody
to share my fire." He took a slurp of salty soup.
"How nice," he said, "to have my soup to myself."

But one night a terrible storm blew up.
The Snorgh was listening to the howl of the
wind when he heard a sound at the door:

Knock!

Knock!

KNOCK!

Knock!

Knock!

KNOCK!

Nobody had ever
knocked at the
Snorgh's door before.
He shuffled over and
opened it just a crack.

Outside in the rain was a bedraggled creature.

"Hello," said the creature. "I'm a sailor. My boat has been washed ashore in the storm. Can I come in?"

"No," said the Snorgh. "Snorghs don't have visitors."

"But you've got such a nice house!" said the sailor, and he marched right in.

He sat down in the Snorgh's chair and warmed his toes by the fire.

The Snorgh harrumphed and went and sat in the bath.

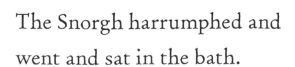

"Mmm! Samphire soup!" said the sailor. "May I?"

"Snorghs don't share soup," said the Snorgh.

But the sailor had already helped himself. **"Delicious!"** he said.

"I'm on an **adventure**," said the sailor. "Do you want to hear about it?"

"No, thank you," said the Snorgh. "Snorghs don't like adventures."

But the sailor told him anyway.
The Snorgh pretended not to listen.

The sailor saved the best story till last.
It was a particularly terrible and
exciting tale about an **island**
that was really a **whale**,

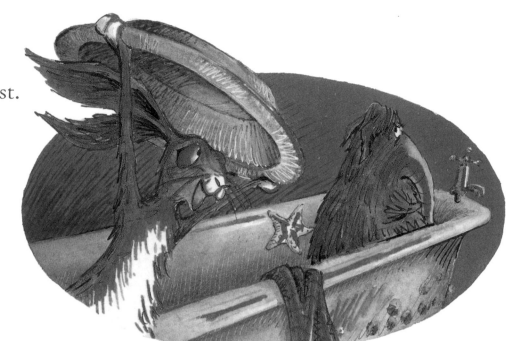

about **whirlwinds**
and waterspouts

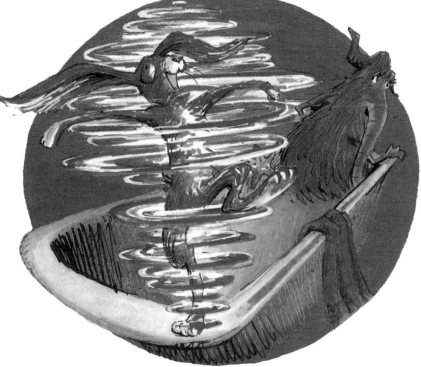

and about a fearsome **sea monster**.

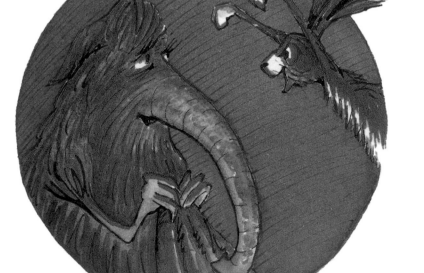

But right in the middle, the clock on the wall struck eight.

# "Bedtime!"

shouted the Snorgh.

"Bedtime?" said the sailor.
"But what about the story?"
"If you have to, you can tell me the
rest in the morning," said the Snorgh.
"Snorghs **always** sleep at eight o'clock."

That night the Snorgh had dreams more **colourful** and **wonderful** than any Snorgh had ever dreamed before.

The Snorgh woke long after the sun had risen.

He felt happier than he could ever remember feeling.
But when he peered out of his bathtub, he saw only his
cold house, his cold fireplace and his pot of cold soup.
The sailor was gone.

"Sailor?" he called. "I'm ready for the rest of the story!"

But the only answer was the lonely moan of the wind.
The Snorgh hurried to the door and peered out.

The beach was deserted.

Then on the horizon he spotted
the tiny triangle of a disappearing sail.
"Sailor!" he shouted. "Wait!
I have to hear the end of the story!"

But the boat just bobbed further away.
"If only I had a boat!" the Snorgh cried.

Then he had an idea . . .

. . . and soon he was paddling
towards the horizon.

"Sailor, wait!" he cried.
"I need to know what happened
to the **whale**!"

When he was far out to sea, he suddenly ran aground.
"Who put that island there?" he muttered.

He clambered out and pushed the
boat back into the water.
"Sailor!" he shouted. "I need to know
what happened with the **whirlwind!**"

He'd just started paddling again, when he
noticed the breeze ruffling his fur.

"Sailor! Wait!" he cried.

"I need to know what the **sea monster** did!"
But his voice was drowned by the wind.

The waves towered higher and higher.

"Sailor!
Where are you?"
the Snorgh cried.

At that moment one enormous
wave picked him up . . .

spun him around . . .

. . . and swept him onto dry land.

The Snorgh peered out
of his bathtub.

And there, by a crackling fire, was the sailor, making soup.
"Hello, Snorgh," said the Sailor. "Are you on an adventure?"
"Absolutely not," said the Snorgh. "Snorghs don't have
adventures. I've just come to hear the end of the story."

"Ah," said the sailor, offering him a bowl of soup.
"But the story hasn't ended yet."
 The Snorgh stamped his foot.

"But I have to know
what happens next!" he cried.
The sailor scratched his chin. "Well, in that case,
you'll just have to come with me. We set sail at dawn."

And what an extraordinary story
it turned out to be!

For Elee – W.B.

For my family – T.D.

First published in 2012 by Alison Green Books

An imprint of Scholastic Children's Books

Euston House, 24 Eversholt Street

London NW1 1DB

A division of Scholastic Ltd

www.scholastic.co.uk

London ~ New York ~ Toronto ~ Sydney ~ Auckland

Mexico City ~ New Delhi ~ Hong Kong

Text copyright © 2012 Will Buckingham

Illustrations copyright © 2012 Thomas Docherty

HB ISBN: 978 1 407116 51 8

PB ISBN: 978 1 407116 52 5

Printed in Singapore

1 3 5 7 9 10 8 6 4 2

The moral rights of Will Buckingham and Thomas Docherty have been asserted.

Papers used by Scholastic Children's Books are made from wood grown in sustainable forests.